Bad Zombie Movie

Level 6G

Written by Lucy George
Illustrated by Sernur Isik
Reading Consultant: Betty Franchi

About Phonics

Spoken English uses more than 40 speech sounds. Each sound is called a *phoneme*. Some phonemes relate to a single letter (d-o-g) and others to combinations of letters (sh-ar-p). When a phoneme is written down, it is called a *grapheme*. Teaching these sounds, matching them to their written form, and sounding out words for reading is the basis of phonics.

Early phonics instruction gives children the tools to sound out, blend, and say the words without having to rely on memory or guesswork. This instruction gives children the confidence and ability to read unfamiliar words, helping them progress toward independent reading.

About the Consultant

Betty Franchi is an American educator with a Bachelor's Degree in Elementary and Middle Education as well as a Master's Degree in Special Education. Betty holds a National Boards for Professional Teaching Standards certification. Throughout her 24 years as a teacher, she has studied and developed an expertise in Phonetic Awareness and has implemented phonetic strategies, teaching many young children to read, including students with special needs.

Reading tips

This book focuses on three sounds made with the letters *ie*; ($\bar{i}$) as in **tie**, ($\bar{e}$) as in **fie**ld, and ($\breve{e}$) as in fr**ie**nd.

Tricky and/or new words in this book

Any words in bold may have unusual spellings or are new and have not yet been introduced.

> ### Tricky and/or new words in this book
>
> **scene one two some
> their four mixture
> action caught**

Extra ways to have fun with this book

After the readers have read the story, ask them questions about what they have just read.

What did Zombie help the friends find?
Who is your favorite character and why?

I think I can capture that Zombie by using this doughnut as bait.

A Pronunciation Guide

This grid contains the sounds used in the stories in levels 4, 5, and 6 and a guide on how to say them.

/ă/ as in pat	/ā/ as in pay	/âr/ as in care	/ä/ as in father
/b/ as in bib	/ch/ as in church	/d/ as in deed/ milled	/ĕ/ as in pet
/ē/ as in bee	/f/ as in fife/ phase/ rough	/g/ as in gag	/h/ as in hat
/hw/ as in which	/ĭ/ as in pit	/ī/ as in pie/ by	/îr/ as in pier
/j/ as in judge	/k/ as in kick/ cat/ pique	/l/ as in lid/ needle (nēd'l)	/m/ as in mom
/n/ as in no/ sudden (sŭd'n)	/ng/ as in thing	/ŏ/ as in pot	/ō/ as in toe
/ô/ as in caught/ paw/ for/ horrid/ hoarse	/oi/ as in noise	/o͝o/ as in took	/ū/ as in cute

/ou/ as in out	/p/ as in pop	/r/ as in roar	/s/ as in sauce
/sh/ as in ship/ dish	/t/ as in tight/ stopped	/th/ as in thin	/th/ as in this
/ŭ/ as in cut	/ûr/ as in urge/ term/ firm/ word/ heard	/v/ as in valve	/w/ as in with
/y/ as in yes	/z/ as in zebra/ xylem	/zh/ as in vision/ pleasure/ garage/	/ə/ as in about/ item/ edible/ gallop/ circus
/ər/ as in butter			

Be careful not to add an /uh/ sound to /s/, /t/, /p/, /c/, /h/, /r/, /m/, /d/, /g/, /l/, /f/ and /b/. For example, say /fff/ not /fuh/ and /sss/ not /suh/.

The cast, crew, and director
are gathered and ready to
start shooting the latest movie,
Bad Zombie Movie.
"Get in your places, everyone,"
shouts the director.

In **scene one**, Auntie is in a field struggling with her heifer.

"Attack now, Zombie!"
shouts the director.

Zombie lumbers into the field. Instead of attacking, he helps Auntie untie her heifer.

In scene **two**, the police
are waiting for a thief.

Zombie is supposed to attack.
Instead of attacking, he helps
the police catch the thief.

In scene three, **some** friends have lost **their** bird.

Zombie is supposed to attack.
Instead he helps the friends
find their bird.

In scene **four**, a niece is baking cookies. Zombie is supposed to attack. Instead of attacking, he helps her stir the **mixture**.

"Zombie! You are supposed to be bad. You have one more chance," shouts the director, who is getting very stressed. "**Action**!"

The police have **caught** the thief.
The friends have found their bird.
Auntie and her niece are sharing
their cookies.

Zombie is supposed to attack
them all. Instead of attacking,
he joins them for a cup of tea.

"Cut!" cries the director.
"Good grief. This is beyond belief.
This movie is called
Bad Zombie Movie.

It's supposed to have a bad zombie in it! Instead, it's just a bad movie." The director storms off the set in disbelief.

OVER **48** TITLES IN SIX LEVELS
Betty Franchi recommends...

Some titles from Level 4

I love reading phonics — **The Circus Mice** — 978 1 84898 783 8

I love reading phonics — **Monster's Night** — 978 1 84898 784 5

I love reading phonics — **Jemima The Spy** — 978 1 84898 785 2

Some titles from Level 5

I love reading phonics — **The Gigantic Bear** — 978 1 84898 787 6

I love reading phonics — **Celebrity Celia** — 978 1 84898 788 3

I love reading phonics — **The Cemetery Dance** — 978 1 84898 789 0

Other titles to enjoy from Level 6

I love reading phonics — **Hugh is New** — 978 1 84898 791 3

I love reading phonics — **Clumsy Eagle** — 978 1 84898 792 0

I love reading phonics — **Owen the Astronaut** — 978 1 84898 794 4

An Hachette Company
First published in the United States by TickTock, an imprint of Octopus Publishing Group.
www.octopusbooksusa.com

Copyright © Octopus Publishing Group Ltd 2013

Distributed in the US by
Hachette Book Group USA
237 Park Avenue, New York NY 10017, USA

Distributed in Canada by
Canadian Manda Group
165 Dufferin Street, Toronto, Ontario, Canada M6K 3H6

ISBN 978 1 84898 793 7

Printed and bound in China
10 9 8 7 6 5 4 3 2 1